If I Were...

with pictures by Doris Otto
and verses by Lene Hille-Brandts
adapted by Elisabeth Duckworth

 CHILDRENS PRESS, CHICAGO

LENE HILLE-BRANDTS wrote a number of books before her death in 1958. Although few of these were published during her lifetime, ten of her books are now in print. Two of these, *The Little Black Hen* and *Guess What* are published in the United States by Childrens Press.

DORIS OTTO is a free-lance illustrator of children's books. In addition to her initial training at the Munich Academy of Arts, she has also studied in France, England, Italy, and Switzerland. Her work has been entered in many large exhibitions in Munich.

Original title: Wenn ich ein kleiner Daumling war
Copyright ⓒ by Annette Betz, München, 1966
EnglishTranslation Copyright ⓒ by W. & R. Chambers, Ltd.,Edinburgh, 1968
New Text Copyright ⓒ 1969 by Regensteiner Publishing Enterprises, Inc.

American Edition Published 1969 by
Regensteiner Publishing Enterprises, Inc.
All Rights Reserved   Printed in U.S.A.
Published Simultaneously in Canada

If I Were...

If I were a lion
That sat beside the ink,
I could watch my father
Work and write and think.
His words come from the inkwell,
So if I took a drink,
Would I be a writer
Or a lion full of ink?

If I were a magician
And in a position
To make dolls dance and hop,

I would also be able
To turn from the table
And make the dancers stop.

If I were an ermine, a weasel, a stoat,
I would be able to change my coat.
Brown for the summer, they have found,
Helps them hide against the ground.
But in their snowtime coat of white,
They are almost out of sight.

If I were a fisherman
And had a block of wood,
I'd use it for a sailing boat,
To leave my neighborhood.
Far at sea I'd drop my line
And never think it odd
To pull aboard my sailing ship
A great big wooden cod.

If I were out in a snowstorm
And stood very still in one place,
I soon would be covered with snowflakes
On my arms and my legs and my face.
I'd look just like a snowman
For everyone to see.
No one would know the snowman
Was really only me.

If I were a king in a golden crown,
I'd march my soldiers up and down.
I wouldn't pretend with a barnyard hen
But have an army of very brave men,
For who in the world would be afraid
Of funny chickens on parade?

If I were a lady,
A make-believe lady,
With hat down over my nose,
You would know without staring
That I was wearing
Some of my mother's clothes.

If I were the wind, you could hear me puff
And whistle and blow at least hard enough
To send the fall leaves all twirling down –
Yellow and orange and dark red and brown.

If I were a giant
Tremendously tall,
Everyone else
Would seem very small.
I would reach for the stars
In the sky every night
So that each of my friends
Could carry a light.

If I were very, very small,
Say just about two inches tall,
I'm sure no insect, bird, or bee
Would ever be afraid of me;
And in a meadow I would lie
And rock a yellow butterfly.

If I were a witch, you know what I'd do?
I'd stir up a magical witches' brew.
I'd give the ghosts and goblins a drink
So they would appear, quick as a wink.
And on Halloween night when all was dark
I'd give them a party in the park.

If I were riding a train puffing steam
Instead of drinking my cocoa with cream,
I'd see faraway mountains and cities and plains
And people on other passenger trains.
I'd travel until there was no more track–
And then, of course, I would have to come back.

If I were a northern Eskimo
Snug in fur from **head** to toe,
I could laugh and sing and play.
Instead of bathing every day,
I would be free to go to sea
And spear a lovely fish for me.

If I were a mountain goat way up here,
There would be nothing for me to fear.
I would not cry or fret or frown
Wondering how a goat gets down.